Blessed With Poetry

Michelle Smith

Michelle Smith
Website: www.blessedwritings.com
Facebook: Blessed with Poetry
Instagram: Blessed.with.Poetry
Email: blessedwritings2019@gmail.com

Copyright © (2018) by Michelle Smith

ISBN – 978-0-9854489-9-8
Library of Congress Control Number 2019908379
Blessed With Poetry
Written by: Michelle Smith
Publishing by: Exposed Books Publishing
Text Formation by: Exposed Books Publishing and Michelle Smith
Cover Design by: Oliva ProDesigns
Printed in the United States of America
Website: www.blessedwritings.com

Acknowledgements

I would like to thank God for his understanding power. God provided me with the mind to understand, so I could complete this book.

Thank you to my husband Greg and to my two sons Gavin and Lil Greg for having patience with me. Thank you to my daughter Maci for your encouraging words and your help. Thank you Mother for being the woman you are. You are a special lady who loves the Lord. I learned how to pray and how to lean on God from you. Thank you for introducing me to church at an early age which lead me to be the person I am today. At 92 you are still going strong and blessed by God. I love you Mom.

I would also like to thank my family and friends for all of their love and support. To my friends that gave me the courage to believe that this book is a blessing and needed to be shared with others, thank you. I also would like to thank my Pastor, Dr. Carl Solomon for teaching the word in such a powerful way. Thank you to all of the preachers and teachers that I have come across who words encouraged me to start and complete this book.

Lord, please bless everyone who reads this book. Allow them to have the ears to hear, a mind to listen and the courage to spread the word.

This books is dedicated
to my mother,
Dorothy Garland.

A Miracle Is Going To Happen

You should always be in fellowship with others who believe in
Christ,
someone who will pray and encourage you in spite of your past life.

In spite of all the things you have done or will do,
and will tell you the truth to help you through.

It is good to be in the company of believers to build
your faith,
the more you're in fellowship, the harder it is for your faith to
break.

There are gifts you will receive from fellowshipping with Christ,
 it will help you to be more equipped to fight.

So please don't come to church just looking for friends,
because some church folks don't even have good sense.

God has you in church to build you up,
to fight a good fight and to stay in touch.

With believers that are willing to help you fight your way through,
 not the ones who will talk you down a notch or two.

God's miracle will also help you with your assignment,
just trust and let God lead you through all your time spent.

Time well spent with God and others who believe in Christ,
who will pray and pray for you to beat the fight.

A miracle is absolutely on its way, so God needs you to prepare,
for a celebration of a lifetime so listen with care.

Blessed With Poetry

See, Peter did nothing to receive this treatment,
thrown in jail and put to death was their intention.

But God had other plans for a miracle was about to happen,
as his church friends prayed for God's connection.

1st Corinthians 12 and 12 states, "though the body has many
different parts,"
they all work together as one body of Christ, we are taught.

I'm a Christian but I can't do it without the body of the church,
it all works together especially when you're hurt.

The church is the resource bank, where we go to refill,
to find whatever the Father has for us we have to sit still.

And if you surround yourself with one or two, to help you fight the
fight,
you can conquer anything that stands in your sight.

They put Peter in the darkest part of the jail,
with guards all around him is what I can tell.

But the church at Mary's just prayed and prayed,
that's the body coming together, that's those saved folks I say.

The folks that will drop on their knees and pray for you,
even if it seems like prayer is not the way it's true.

Now, God had plans and this miracle was about to happen,
not just for Peter, but also for the church for they knew Peter was
captured.

God sent an angel to get Peter you know,
he woke him and told him "get up lets go."

Blessed With Poetry

See, you need to get dress and go where God is taking you,
and dress like that miracle that you know is your breakthrough.

This text is not just about Peter, but everyone in fellowship with
Christ,
the praying church at Mary's house is an example of the
connection...that's tight.

As Peter walked pass the guards the chains began to fall,
Peter was thinking this must be a dream that's all.

When he realized he was out he went straight to Mary's door,
knocked and knocked then Rhoda heard his voice.

"It's Peter" she shouted and was excited to hear,
but they didn't believe that what she heard was really clear.

Now as they say an unknown person opened the door,
but the blessings didn't come until they opened it for sure.

So just know that your miracle is about to come,
just be in fellowship with believers that are one.

One in the spirit and with the body of Christ,
for that miracle might only knock for you once or twice.

Ephesians 6:10-18

I'm About That Life

See you have to be about that life that God has promised you,
so stand strong in the faith that God has given to you.

Although the enemy is out to take your life,
willing to use you as his sacrifice.

Whether you know it or not you are always at war,
against all the evil tactics from the devil for sure.

The battle is to help you grow further they tell us,
you can't have the good without the bad so let's stay focus.

Yes, the devil is sneaky and he will attack,
he will take you up close as a matter of fact.

You won't see him in that so called movie form,
a red cape, a pitchfork not even horns.

But, he will be around and close for sure,
he will be in a place that is known of course.

Like in Genesis he appeared as a snake you see,
but what's a snake to a gardener but a familiar face indeed.

You should know the devil would try to come for you,
as long as your following God he is in war against you.

The life that you live will be attacked,
as long as we stay on a straight and narrow path.

But, know that this battle is to help you grow stronger, just hold on
and wear your own armor.

Remember put on that armor of the Lord you see,
for every piece of that armor will protect you and me.

Blessed With Poetry

Just because you don't see the attack,
doesn't mean you're free from all the crap.

Look, you can't see the flu coming but it will attack for sure,
and when it gets you, it will bring you down and then some more.

See, Ephesians 6:1-6 is telling you what you should do,
but then verse 10-18 tells you to protect what's true.

He says stay strong in the Lord because he is by your side,
you can't stand alone because that my dear, just won't fly.

God will be there even if you don't feel so strong,
he will protect you and that is why you will never be alone.

Your bills will get paid, things will surely happen,
that job you wanted it will come in close caption.

But don't forget everything comes with something you know,
the devil will temp you while you are standing for Christ, and that's
low.

But, that better job, that new business came with those old friends
of course,
who will not like you going forward and want to bring you down
for sure.

Again I say, the devil will be after you and will come up close,
that is why that armor is built for close attacks the most.

Stand firm with the buckle around your waist,
and with the breastplate of righteousness in its place.

Your feet they are planted and ready you see,
that my dear is the gospel that will give you peace.

And that shield, you know that shield of faith,
it will get you through the battle of life that the devil try's to take.

This shield is needed because the advisory will come from within,
he will always be on your team you know them, Amen.

See, when the church is attacked, it's attacked from within,
the one trying to tear that ministry down, you know it's usually your friend.

So put on that whole armor and not just a part,
you need all of it to fight your attacks near and far.

And don't worry, stand strong because God has your back,
remember God's words to Peter as a matter of fact.

"Upon this rock I will build my church and all power in hell will not conquer it."

That's God saying "as long as you serve me I have this under control,"
no more words needed in this poem Lord I'm yours!

Philippians
2:3-4

Lord Bless My Friends

Lord I ask that you, "bless my friends,"
watch over them as no one else can.

Bless their heart, their soul and their mind,
touch any hurt and pain you might find.

Bless their lives in a special way,
that they all will be happy and free someday.

I might not see their pain and they may hide their hurt,
but deep down inside I know they put you first.

They may question their actions and where they might be,
but everything happens for a reason and they need to believe.

I believe that all the pain and hurt that they may feel,
will one day be erased and they will be healed.

Their life will be happy and they will find their joy,
maybe a new life, a new beginning, they will find so much more.

My love for them is deeper than they may ever know,
my prayers for them are stronger, much stronger than gold.

But, still I know it can only come from you,
the joy in their life is what's overdue.

So keep them in mind as they may suffer some,
as they will one day stand and rise in the face of everyone.

They will rest and will find a peace of mind,
in this lifetime with your prayers and mine.

2nd Kings

5:3

The Messenger

Many of us are not where we want to be,
many of us don't have things that are meant for thee.

Some of us complain and some of us know,
we are not open to just letting things flow.

See, one of the reasons we are not where we should,
is because we won't step out of our comfort zone as we could.

And my God this same spirit as you will,
has compelled the church as we just sit still.

We have allowed this spirit to come in and take over things,
we do nothing and allow it to control things with shame.

You know you've seen it in church for sure,
that person you ignored because her dress was too short.

That young man whose pants are hanging too far down,
that man who had an odor and you look at him with a frown.

See, if someone comes into the church and they don't look the same,
we ignore what they say; we don't even let them explain.

If their clothes are not in-tact and their hair is not straight,
we tend to look at them with such disgrace.

But my God in this season, God is making a change,
God is using common people to lead and explain.

These common folks you know might not be able to sang,
these common folks might wear clothes that seem to be lame.

But they will have a message for you and for me,
and that message may just set us free.

2nd Kings introduces us to Naaman you know,
he was victorious in fighting in the Kings army as so.

But, through all of his battles and all of his wins,
Naaman had leprosy that he was dealing with within.

Even with leprosy he continued to fight,
this was his assignment he did with all his might.

How many of us have faced problems and still succeed,
for if it's God's assignment then nothing can intercede?

This is God's grace, good for you and for me,
this grace that God gives will surely help you succeed.

We can push through and do what God has given us to do,
with problems or sickness he will see us through.

Now see this leprosy was supposed to keep Naaman down,
but Naaman fought through it with grace and not a frown.

But, then this maid or may I say a messenger you see,
made one statement that would change his way of life indeed.

"I wish my master would go to see the prophet in Samaria, for he
would heal his leprosy."

That one statement coming from this little girl,
was more powerful than anyone had ever heard.

This girl never said might or I think the prophet will heal,
she said, "My master will be healed."

Blessed With Poetry

See, there was no doubt in her mind that Naaman would be healed,
so she spoke it out loud so her mistress would hear.

That common little girl was the messenger for him,
we don't know her name but her statement sends chills.

For not the king or Naaman's wife, not even his friends,
gave a message that would heal him from within.

Yet you do realize some people may not want you to be healed,
some people are ok with you not being fulfilled.

But you may never know who your messenger might be,
that common guy or gal that looks suspicious you see.

So do me a favor, step out of your confront zone,
choose people that can make a difference, don't judge based on
their clothes.

You don't even know who God may use to send you a word,
the one you may least expect is what I've heard.

So let's not shy away from people you think might not play the part,
for they might be the one who will touch your heart.

You will make it and God will give you grace,
just don't let that common person with the special message get
away.

1ˢᵗ Samuel

17:38-45

What Works For You Won't Work For Me

We are familiar and know the story of David and Goliath,
whenever there is an underdog this story always arises.

The small and weak going up against something big and strong,
oh my, may we say that it is just so wrong.

But, then it's wonderful and exciting to see the underdog win,
we love to see them on top time and time again.

In this story it's not the adult but the child who wins,
not a child of the world but a child in God's wings.

You see, David teaches us that whenever we go against a giant we
have to go with what works,
don't think too much, just let your heart lead first.

All of us will go against a giant or giants I may say,
but you can't handle every giant in the same way.

What may work for me may not work for you,
you might not even know what to do.

But you can't take advice from others to have your problems solved,
ask the Lord to give you a plan to work on your family, your
finances, your marriage that's all.

See, Saul put his armor on David and gave him some advice,
but David knew this advice just didn't feel right.

The breastplate and the head armor was what Saul knew,
but David did not want to fight with something new.

Blessed With Poetry

David was a worshiper of God and soon a warrior of truth,
he worshiped God and knew his life was blessed through and
through.

In verse 39 David said, "I cannot go in this,"
it was all too much and he just wasn't used to it.

David was telling us to just go with what works for you,
not what works for someone else, wow I just laugh because this is
true.

How often do we take advice from others on what to do,
all the while knowing within our hearts what God is telling us to do.

So don't think that big person on your job knows what to do,
for their advice my dear may not be for you.

David always had his staff and his stones,
the tools from his past are what made him strong.

You know the struggles behind you can give you strength,
when you use it in the future with confidence.

See shepherds never leave without their staff,
this staff was a comfort to David and also from his past.

Just know the Holy Spirit has been with you in your past,
this my dear is all you need, just carry your own staff.

And David stones they were there to fight things far away,
the stones are the prayers we use to fight our battles with every day.

David wasn't afraid as he told Goliath "I come in the name of the
Lord of heaven's army," you see,
those words were David's strength and armor it was complete.

Blessed With Poetry

From there David picked up five smooth stones,
that and his staff was all he needed, for he wasn't alone.

Far as we know Gods army was behind him as he started to swing,
moving forward as he was comfortable with what God would bring.

There is something that will work with your pain and your hurt all
the time,
you may feel your frustration rising but God has you, just let your
light shine.

Come to God with confidence for you know it worked before,
God will lead you again and again, God will carry your sword.

So always go with whatever works for you and not for anyone else,
kill that giant and trust in God because having faith will always
help.

Acts

8:4~8

Joy In The City

Acts is the book of history I'm told,
also to be appreciated for the blue print of what the church should uphold.

Chapter 8 says how a believer and a Christian can have real joy,
the joy that comes from loving the word and the joy from loving the Lord.

If you have joy in your life, the plan is realized,
that God has a plan for the church and also for your life.

You know you have to be prepared for agitation that comes from Satan,
for God is preparing us for what has to be taken.

He has to take us from being so comfortable you see,
to show us the life that he has for you and for me.

This chapter moves the people from Jerusalem to Samara,
the people of Samara had joy instead of terror.

So don't get mad when agitation comes,
because God is moving you to another place my son.

Elevation of the Saints is a part of God's holy plan,
for the Saints to speak the word to all in God's land.

For if you do not move you will never see,
the plan God has in store for thee.

Satan wanted to destroy the church but God allowed it to grow,
so just remember with your every move God has control.

Blessed With Poetry

So tell his word and set the people free,
for the one who accepts the word will need you and me.

Phillip was once a deacon and then he became a preacher,
because God moved him from his comfort zone to become a leader.

God has given us all a gift,
but we must move to another place to allow it to shift.

To shift into what God has in store for us,
but we will never know this gift if God didn't allow some stuff.

Now, if you're in this looking to get a pat on your back,
think again my friend for that's not where it's at.

We should spread our gifts to bring people to Christ,
let The Lord lead you and guide you and show you what's right.

But, when you reject God, you cannot have joy,
yet when you accept him in your life you will have joy for sure.

Now, knowing that we are here by God's good grace,
should make you want to testify and show people God's way.

The gospel should be taught for the people to see,
the miracles and the signs that are shown you must agree.

Every time I turn around I'm blessed indeed,
over and over I can't began to perceive.

That there is joy that is given by his grace,
although this world has given God so much hate.

Spread the word and let God take you to that joyful place,
the city of joy that we all can one day face.

Blessed With Poetry

Let's be elevated and let your light shine,
remember God is in front, so leave Satan behind.

Show your joy from one place to the next,
for God's holy plan is what you should expect.

Proverbs

16

God's Way

We can plan our life or path the way that we want,
but God has the answer we surely don't.

Take your plan of action to God and leave it there,
for his purpose and decisions will be in our best care.

The wicked man, yes he will have his day,
for God gives us all a chance, even the ones without faith.

So, don't get above yourself and forget who you are,
because God will and has always been with you this far.

When you fear the Lord he keeps you in peace,
no evil will come to you, for your enemies will drop to your feet.

Speak kind words and never speak evil of others,
for God loves a positive tongue so do not bash your brother.

We may try to lead ourselves because we think it's right,
but evil will come if we don't let God guide us through the fight.

I would rather have wisdom from God than silver and gold,
knowing God's wisdom is pleasing to him I'm told.

So you should live your life humble and speak well of everyone,
for a wise man will speak wise, as it is pleasing to God and his son.

It might bring gray hairs but I'm proud to say,
it's my glory and gain to live in God's holy way.

So when you make plans for your life it's safe to say,
that God has the last word no matter how your path might sway.

John

5:2

The Feast Or The Field

This was a day when 3 holy days or feast were required for Jews,
to acknowledge the festivities and to be holy and true.

But, for some odd reason on the way to the feast,
Jesus was drawn to this pool of the lame and needy.

For Jesus was drawn to this man that laid on a mat,
for 38 years as a matter of fact.

Jesus asked the man a question, "Do you want to be healed?"
His answer was lame as he gave excuses and squealed.

As Jesus began to do his work in the field,
his disciples didn't notice him missing for the feast was all they
could feel.

But, that didn't matter as Jesus began to do his work,
on the man that was lying on his back and trembling with hurt.

So let's ask the question, "How did Jesus go there?"
Instead of going to the feast he went to work and share.

To share his miracles on the ones in need,
not the ones at the feast for they were good indeed.

See, we church folks have to wonder,
do we want to work in the field or eat at the feast?

For the feast that's the church, but where do we feed,
the ones who are hungry and need to be set free?

You know the field is where we should share God's word to others,
for the ones at the feast don't care or even bother.

Blessed With Poetry

To share Gods word after they feast about what they have heard,
and they don't even share with sinners, which is really absurd.

Then you ask, "What makes the church more than a church?"
Is it the feast that we eat then go to the field to work and search?

Search for the ones who need to hear,
what God has for them and feel that God is real.

Is there a connection to worshipping God in the church,
and going out in to the field to do God's work?

See, we seem to celebrate in church and not do the fieldwork,
for in church we are different with those that know our hurt.

But it's time to go out and share in the field,
to the folks who don't understand Jesus and why we are here.

Don't gather in church to get strength and then become weak,
for that strength that lies within will help everyone see.

But, the thing I don't understand is why no one noticed that Jesus
was missing,
if they followed him closely they would have been beside him as he
witnessed.

Just imagine if everyone would have went to the field
to celebrate life,
then everyone would have been healed.

Then the feast would have come to an unfamiliar place,
to celebrate life and to heal for Christ's sake.

So, remember when the benediction in church is over,
that doesn't mean you don't go to the field and spread the word
from shoulder to shoulder.

Blessed With Poetry

For God's assignment for you is to go to the field,
to show God's work and let the people see that God can heal.

Now, as Jesus talked with the man all he heard was complaints,
about how he couldn't get to the water and others took his place.

Is that how we are, we let frustration get us down,
watching others elevate as we began to frown?

Instead of rolling into the water or dragging himself in,
he just sat and waited for others. Wow, the pity he felt within.

Do you feel pity as you sit on your mat?
Instead of fighting to get yourself from this place to that.

See God gives us chances to do what we're supposed to do,
and not lie on your back and wait for others to come to you.

See, the man was on the mat one-week and walking the next,
that was a miracle in its self and that's a fact.

Just think about it and look at what this means,
how quickly things can change if you follow God's lead.

So stop complaining and get out in the field to do Gods work,
for the festivities won't last long and your life will still hurt.

So, goodbye because I'm going to the field to make it known,
that Jesus can heal and will be coming back soon.

Romans
8:37

The Winning Team

Reading this scripture I have to say "Thank you Lord" for letting
me know the love of God.

See, this scripture should be comforting to know,
that God loves us and sent Jesus to help us grow.

When we think of the church we think of the building as so,
but as Christians we should be the church the world should know.

Paul talks about us representing Christ,
because we all should be believers and live Christ like.

When you are a believer you are a member of the church,
everyone should see the Christ in you even when life hurts.

See, it's not the fact that we go to church that should set us apart,
it's the love of Christ in us that the world should see from a far.

Far and beyond what we can imagine,
the pain of things in our life should not even matter.

For we know that God has our back,
this scripture makes it clear as a matter of fact.

When you are a part of the kingdom you are with him,
it doesn't matter how bad it may seem you will always win.

God can heal you from whatever you're going through,
the love my dear that he shows us is true.

See, to be connected to God means you are on the winning team,
but to be a part you must accept Jesus Christ you see.

Blessed With Poetry

Jesus said "I am the way the truth and the light,"
and there is no church without believing in Christ.

There is no way for you to get to God without Christ,
this is the message if you want this life.

We live in a society where everything is right now,
fix it please, with no time allowed.

Some people say yes to Jesus because they are going through,
at the time it sounds good because you think God will take care of
you.

Not knowing that Jesus is not here to free you from every problem,
but to know he will help you through so that you can solve them.

Like Simon, Jesus let the devil come in,
but Jesus prayed for Simon and that is when his strength began.

The thorn in Paul's side, God let stay,
God let him suffer a little but showed him the way.

Some people go through all types of situations but God see's it all,
he will be there to comfort you when you fall.

See, no matter what you face you will conquer it all,
you are more than a conqueror and that should make you stand tall.

God wants you to win in this life,
because you are a part of God's shining light.

It might look discouraging and some things will get you down,
for weeping may endure for a night but the morning will come
around.

So remember in order to get to God you have to go through Christ,
even Acts 4 and 12 will show you this twice.

Blessed With Poetry

You cannot have salvation without being saved,
and you can't get to God without Jesus Christ just the same.

So, if you want to be on the winning team,
put God in your life by letting Christ intervene.

Now get your attitude right and understand,
that God is the winning team and not nearly an earthly man.

2 Corinthians

12: 1 - 10

What Bothers You Could Bless You

We know Paul as a great disciple,
we are able to track his ministry throughout the bible.

We come to know him as a major man of faith,
showing his true faith no matter what it takes.

Paul was not perfect for he was just a man,
but bold in his faith for that was in God's plan.

Paul planted seeds in the church that we use today,
his quotes and his sayings leads us in a good way.

The way that God intends for us to grow,
through pain and suffering we will surely know.

Know our strength and weakness through our pain,
because it's there for a reason, we will call out God's name.

One thing we've learned from Paul is that God will supply all our needs,
and we can take that to heart, for our past shows us indeed.

"All things work together for them that love The Lord,"
is another reason Paul has given us to search God for.

Paul gave us these words through his own testimony,
because he was living in the spirit and he was never lonely.

Paul didn't just talk about the spirit; he shared with us his experience,
so we may know his struggle with no interference.

Paul's message was clear and he was encouraged by faith,
but tell me have you thanked God for all your mistakes.

Blessed With Poetry

Paul was blessed but yet had a thorn bothering him,
but no one knew if the thorn was sickness or a bad limb.

Yet, we know Paul asked God three times to remove it you see,
we also know Paul understood and said "thank God for the pain in
me."

Through it all Paul had to remember to have faith in thee,
for the thorn was a small hindrance of pain indeed.

When you look back over your life what do you see,
all the blessings God has given to you and to me.

But, my God do you realize how small the thorn is,
compared to the blessings in store for you ahead.

We always seem to say, "We are praying about it,"
but we are just venting hoping God will remove us from it.

God answers our prayers according to his purpose and will,
so always thank God, wait and stand still.

Paul's background shows us he was against the church,
but that didn't matter because God saw his heart first.

What does this mean for you and me?
That our past doesn't matter for God will set us free.

So thank God for that thorn you have but sometimes cannot see,
for there is a blessing that God has in store for you and me.

Some answers show light for others to deliverer,
to deliver God's word, to share and to be a giver.

We are looking for God to always answer us in works,
we are thinking, "My God this thorn surely hurts."

God may also show it to us in words and dialog,
but when you least expect it, he will answer your call.

So, take that small thorn for what it is,
become stronger through your pains and all your fears.

Stand still and be strong and listen for it is true,
"What bothers you may also be a blessing for you."

2 Corinthians

4: 1-6

When You See Glory For Yourself

Glory, my dear is the way God reveals himself to you,
to let you know who you are and that his word is true.

See in Acts chapter 9, Paul was one of the perfect examples of
God's exposure,
while on his way to Damascus to get Christians and turn them over.

Turn them over to Jerusalem and make them prisoners you see,
My God this was his only mission to fight the mission of thee.

Then, after God had exposed himself to Paul,
Paul began to serve God and that was the beginning of it all.

Once you see God and see him truly for who he is,
there is no way back from God's grip I hear.

Now, after the encounter Paul seemed to be blind for three days,
until he spoke to Ananias who showed him the way.

The Lord told Ananias that Saul who was now Paul,
was the chosen one and must suffer for my namesake that's all.

So Ananias told Saul that the Lord will appear again,
and something fell from Saul's eyes and it was on from then.

Saul was baptized and then gained his strength,
he then spent time with the disciples and the preaching began.

Now that's another story so let's get back to The Church of
Corinthian,
where Paul was bold in serving the Lord and not his friends.

Blessed With Poetry

Now Paul was there at the Corinthian Church to serve even though
his spirit was hurt,
because the people were not serving God or giving thanks to the
Lord in this church.

See, ministry my dear is very hard work,
while serving God you cannot be a jerk.

This is a calling and is not for no wimps,
for every officer in the church should be there to honor him.

So, don't quit a ministry when someone don't like you, you see,
you are not there to serve them but the Lord and thee.

Now, Paul went through a lot and even almost died,
but that didn't stop his love for Jesus and that made me cry.

Paul was bit by a snake they even threw stones at him to name few,
of some of the things that Paul had gone through.

But, do you think he quit or regret serving God on high,
this my dear is why we should serve God with pride.

We are not serving officers of the church and we are not wimps,
we are chosen to serve God and can't afford for no foolish attempts.

To have people stop us from serving God and from setting us free,
so don't back down from people who are stupid and don't agree.

Some of these people will stand up and only tell,
not the things of God but only talk of themselves.

These people will talk about themselves and put the word on the
shelf,
I guess they seem to think that the word won't help.

But you know you can't preach without saying something about God and Jesus works,
and to not talk about the resurrection would really hurt.

So don't stop preaching or teaching, ushering or singing or even coming to church,
because Gods mercy is what got you out of all your real hurt.

Look, even though the church of Corinthians was not teaching God's word,
Paul didn't give up on the truth or telling God's word.

He stayed in a place and served where he did not like,
to make sure God's word was to be heard, he stayed for the fight.

To fight the ones who were only trying to lift themselves,
he stayed to fight for their souls and to give them help.

He wanted to help others despite of his past,
he was a man who knew God's word would last and last.

Paul's encounter with God was his testimony, his truth and what he saw,
but his encounter with Jesus is what got him this far.

Paul wasn't the one, who saw Jesus works face to face,
but he encountered the Lord and that showed him the way.

So believe me when you know Jesus and is exposed to his faith,
nothing will make you stop worshipping God and showing the people the way.

Now know your glory and your encounter with Jesus my friend,
please get to know God and serve only as you can.

Esther

4:12-1 &

5:1-2

The Woman That Makes It Happen

God made everything from heaven to earth,
he's my God, my friend whose mercy saves me from hurt.

He is a God, who doesn't need any of my help,
my advice, my perspective or my two cents, I do not need to yelp!!

He alone is my God and his will, will be done,
for my God is real and the only one.

Who can help you and me during our time of need?
His love and mercy will free us indeed.

Yet sometimes God's will, we might not like so much,
but sometimes we need his anointing touch.

See, God will push us to places we don't want to go,
and when we get there we realize how blessed we are though.

We might be struck down, hurt and even feeling alone,
but then we realize that God has never left us as it is shown.

Every time we think or feel like it's the end,
God steps in on time you know it my friend.

We are strong enough to notice that things happen for a reason,
and that God allows it to happen for us to get through that season.

For example, Joseph knew the pain of being favored by God,
being hated by people from near and far.

But, Joseph was a survivor and that my dear is true,
through the fight and the pain he knew God was the truth.

Even through this story of Esther, God is not mentioned you see,
but he is definitely around, as you will receive.

Blessed With Poetry

Such power God has even when he is not mentioned,
he shows up anyway during our time of tension.

See, Esther was beautiful and showed up at the right time,
when The King was looking for a queen to pass the time by.

Remember, sometimes you are put in a place God intends for you to be,
and when the time comes the test will be complete.

Now, out of all the women Esther was the one the king favored,
for her beauty alone, her attractiveness was his flavor.

In this position that Esther was deemed to be in,
when the announcement came to kill the Jew she fit right in.

To be right in the place to fulfill a task,
that was meant for her, it was to come true at last.

Mordecai was afraid and was hurting for his people,
then leaned on Esther who stood in the kings steeple.

But, instead of Esther being afraid of losing her position,
Esther stepped out on faith with no hesitation as it is mentioned.

She told Mordecai, "Go tell the others to fast for 3 days,
as I and my servants will do just the same."

Then after the 3 days Esther went to the king,
with God on her side she was a brave little thing.

See, we as woman do a lot as you can see,
we are brave and strong and will try to do everything.

But we are not superwoman and sometimes we need to fold,
let God take over and lead us to our goal.

Blessed With Poetry

Whether we are tall, short, rich, poor or in a powerful position or not,
we are sometimes used exactly where we stand, right there in that spot.

Just imagine, going to the king unannounced and with a goal,
she did what God said and God was already in control.

Remember, we have to step out on faith and let God lead,
for the position you are in God put you there for a need.

So, listen to God and step out for it will be okay,
remember to trust and let him lead the way.

It will put you on top and no others can bring you down,
if you just realize that God is always around.

Every word Jesus said on the cross God made it happen,
Jesus suffering and even him forgiving others is all that mattered.

Jesus was betrayed and beaten yet still did what he was told,
he saves us from sin and saves our souls.

See, in this story it doesn't matter how far God can take you,
just step out and believe how God can still save you.

From the fall you may see things going downhill,
but it's not that your falling, God just wants you to listen to him.

Dare to be the woman that makes the change,
dare to listen and to try not to explain.

Just go on in life and listen closely to God,
even when you think he's not mentioned, he's never too far.

Psalms

23

Through The Valley

This particular scripture David leads us to know,
that God is our protector, provider and guidance for sure.

God leads us in the righteous direction for our souls,
then gives us time to rest as we grow.

But, this scripture not only tells us that God is the way,
he lets us know what happens even if we go astray.

Even if we stray we keep his love,
he will renew our strength that comes from above.

So just think, to lie down in green pastures you know,
the road is tough, but the spirit of God will lighten the load.

This means he also gives us time to rest,
time to heal in a place of comfort that makes us blessed.

He leads us beside the still waters as you can see,
he calms our troubled minds and allows us to breathe.

But God doesn't just restore us for ourselves in need,
he restores us for his namesake that's true indeed.

For if God will restore us then we can proclaim righteousness to others,
in Jesus name we will spread the word to our sisters and brothers.

So when walking through the valley of the shadow of death,
how can we be afraid of anything along our steps?

Even in the shadow there's a light that will always shine,
for you cannot have a shadow without light every time.

Blessed With Poetry

So, don't think that the darkness is just darkness that you see,
for God is the light that is shining to protect you and me.

That is how we should know that God is with us all,
because not only is he light but his rod also protects our fall.

God is the only one, who can follow us through the valley as so,
and as long as he is with us we will never fall below.

Below the sin, that we cannot even see,
the table that's being prepared for you and me.

And I don't know about you but I have a goal,
to fight my way through, to get to my table of love you know.

Can you imagine that table that waits on the other end,
in the presence of our enemies and even some of our friends?

But, because our head is anointed with oil,
we will always fall on our father's gracious soil.

My God I have to say, "Thank you, thank you so much,"
because this scripture shows me you love me and I am touched.

What a feeling to know God, you will be with me where ever I go,
and will never flee from me is what this scripture shows.

You are my Shepherd, my glory Devine,
it doesn't matter the sin, you always rescued me every time.

Thank you David for showing me your strength,
that God gave to you over and over again.

So, let God guide you through the darkness of life,
let God protect you and show you the marvelous light.

1 Corinthians 13:4-7

God's Love

This letter from Paul defines real love,
for the Corinthians needed to know the true love from above.

See love is not boastful, jealous or proud,
love will conquer over evil every single time.

This letter teaches us to love people and give them hope,
even the ones who make you angry and treat you like dirt.

When you think on it, you can't do wrong and God not forgive,
so, why should you hold on to the bad things that people have did?

God doesn't look out at our past and then say "No,"
He forgives us in the future and that is no joke.

He looks beyond any faults and even his pain,
and gives us life that we will never be able to explain.

We as humans seem not to forgive on our own,
but being closer to God can help us as it has shown.

Like the thief on the cross that Jesus forgave,
"you will be with me in heaven," is what my Lord said.

Now you know there was no way Jesus was thinking of the thieves
sinful past,
when he gave his life to Christ his past no longer last.

This, my dear shows us the way,
how God forgives us no matter what others may say.

God never loses faith and is hopeful in us,
that we might see what's ahead and our past sins he won't touch.

Because God starts from the time you asked him to come in,
so why can't we forgive others for their past sins.

You know I can't believe it when I think of this letter,
Paul said, "God will always love us and life will get better."

Through every circumstance God has always come through,
and when you think of your life you know this to be true.

So, be kind to others even when they have done you wrong,
show love not hate because love conquers through it all.

God says I won't give up on you, so you shouldn't give up on
anyone else,
because God's grace is what carried you this far, you were not by
yourself.

Don't forget to praise God now and not just when something is
wrong,
don't wait until that day when your life takes a fall.

The job, the marriage, the money and the pain,
God will always be here even through all the shame.

Because grace is what kept you and will bring you back,
and love is what will heal you and that's a fact.

So be hopeful and love with grace for it will set you free,
for if God can love you than you should be able to love with ease.

Ecclesiastes

3:11

God Is Never Late

Do you wonder sometimes where God is?
Do you look and wonder if he is near?

Times seem hard and we can't explain,
that the issue is just, being a man.

We tend to be stressed out and can't figure our way,
we tend to lean on the wrong ones they say.

But how will we know where to go,
to show our love to God and watch as it grows.

Some sit in church and have a blind eye,
to the real problems that are lurking inside.

Some people come to church and cover up,
the true pain that they have really felt.

But as brothers and sisters we should know,
that if we put it in God's hands we should let it go.

God is good and he makes no mistakes,
so let's give it to God, whatever it takes.

You may look around and it seems as if people don't care,
and that is why most of us tend to not share.

For the fear of being judged or not liked anymore,
the fear of people knowing, that we are bleeding inside for sure.

I tend to wonder what does it take,
to make the love in the church grow and become great.

Blessed With Poetry

Look and see what's going on, the church is falling into a storm,
we all need to find a new home and church is where we belong.

But the storm we have to go through is good you see,
for it is designed to strengthen you and me.

God has a hand in everything his Will shall prevail,
but we have to hold on and wait, for God never fails.

Then when you sit and look back on your life you'll see,
God has never left you and his right hand will set you free.

Life is really hard and lives are broken,
but there is no such thing as divided token.

This issue is not with God as you can tell,
we need to sit down and search deep in ourselves,
for depression and anger is right on our tail.

And when we don't lean on God for his help,
we lose what's right and that's when we can tell.

That we are not walking in the light,
and what we are doing is not truly right.

For when we turn around we will see,
that God is here and he never left you or me.

You realize the question is not if God is too late,
but rather the question is can you wait?

So wait for Gods purpose because it will come for you,
stop running from God, stand still and be true.

He looks outside and he looks straight in,
to your heart and mind he knows what's best in the end.

Genesis

29:30

Having Patience And Strength

The story of Jacob, Leah and Rachel,
starts with a story of plain old being able.

Being able or shall I say having the power to make it through,
making it through whatever God has in store for you.

See, Jacob was a man who knew what he wanted,
his sight was on Rachel to satisfy his hunger.

Hunger for love, lust, want and need,
he knew this encounter would satisfy him indeed.

See, Jacob had no gifts so he worked seven years for Laban,
who promised him Rachel in exchange for his labor.

After seven years Jacob was ready for his reward,
but this had changed for Laban deceived him like a stab with a
sword.

See, Jacob partied the night before,
not knowing that Laban sent Leah to be his toy.

Not knowing he laid with the woman he didn't adore,
he was tricked to work for Rachel seven years more.

Seven more years, My God, to get what he wanted,
that's fourteen altogether his mind begins to ponder.

The question is, would you make this choice,
to wait 14 years for something you have already voiced?

After you've worked hard for it clear and free,
only to learn that it can't be yours for another 7 years indeed.

See, faith will make you bold enough to see,
to see that the next seven years is part of a complete journey.

A complete package that will end in something GREAT,
just continue to hold on to that bold faith.

See Leah bore children that saved you and me,
so those seven years of labor and love still had a meaning.

If you are on a long journey to be free,
just hold on to bold faith because it will help you to see.

That what God has intended for you, it will come in time,
whether you want it or not, it will come and you will be fine.

And it will shine so bright for the world to see,
so realize that seven years was meant for you indeed.

God only gives weight to those he knows who handle,
the bold faith that is given to you in its own specific channel.

Channel meaning the path and that can be a challenge,
but hold on my dear, as I said before he knows what you can
handle.

So be BOLD and wait those years until the work is complete,
because God has a great plan, as you will see.

"WOW! I see it but can you believe it?"

"That everything happens for a reason and disappointments can set
you free."

1 Chronicles

16:11

Strength

This scripture is from David's praise,
for if we worship the Lord and keep our heads raised.

Then this will make praise a continuous thing,
to trust him, love him and claim his name.

I must say when they brought the Ark to that special place,
that David prepared for an offering for God's good grace.

They did a special worship as David appointed others,
to share in God's glory with the men and with others.

The song that David gave was a song of thanksgiving,
for everyone praised God and gave thanks to God's greatness.

But as I came to verse 11, it talks about strength,
I started to wonder, who pondered on this?

I say to everyone that feels like they are in the dumps,
that God won't leave you or throw you out like junk.

For that thing that may be going on in your life that makes you weak,
if you would only trust in God, he will set you free.

At times a feeling may come upon you as if you're missing
something in life I've been told,
as if your life might not even be whole.

That job, that relationship may not seem to be going to well,
maybe the love of your life left you in a spell.

Blessed With Poetry

But, remember for some reason God has chosen you,
to spread the word to others so go and speak the truth.

The decisions you made in life, may not seem right,
but when you think of God's love it will give you the strength to
fight.

Just remember the things God has brought you through,
and remember when you thought the world would end with you.

Remember PLEASE, that God is real,
he feels your hurt and your pain he can heal.

Anytime you think that you may be going through,
do as David did, appoint your friends who are true.

Surround yourself with people that are humble,
and will have your back even if you stumble.

For everyone cannot lead the people and everyone cannot be your
friend,
that's why the role that is given to us is not always common to men.

See, the Levites that David appointed had a certain role,
and they all praised God with their certain gifts I was told.

So, praise God during your down times for he will bring you up,
praise God during your good times to keep in touch.

Praise God for your struggle, for you will make it through,
praise God for your pain because it's only for you.

This struggle will only be for a little while,
and the ones God appoint for you will be by your side.

And this is where your strength will lie,
God will be there for you every time.

"Shout about who you are
and know that God made
you perfect by far."

You Should Know You Are A Star

We all are a work in progress,
but not knowing who you are slows up the process.

When you don't know who you are then you lack confidence,
you may even look stupid and hang around a lot of nonsense.

Some people need you to need them, and that's a sign of bondage,
you give them strength, courage and confidence.

But when you know who you are, you become a real piece of work,
not taking or settling for nonsense from dumb jerks.

See no one can walk, talk and even snap their neck like you,
no one can dress, dance and strut the way you do.

You are somebody so don't talk to dumb folks,
let them watch as you take them on a backstroke.

That backstroke will send them in an uproar,
your authority and confidence will show for sure.

You are living your life like it's golden and everyone will see,
but they just can' t handle the strength that God has brought to thee.

For there is no end to what God can do,
what he has done for others he can do for you.

We are saved for a reason for God has something for us to do,
but our representation will have to show through.

You are a wonder to be hold and everything about you is a
testimony,
people can look and tell that this joy cannot be phony.

Blessed With Poetry

Your value is based on the one, who made you,
the same God that made the world perfect has made you too.

There will never be a person made just like you,
your nose, hands, feet and even your eyes my Boo.

We have been saved by redemption, as you know is true,
but Sin can corrupt integrity in me and in you.

Self-inflicted nonsense is the word SIN,
we seem to destroy ourselves from within.

Since God made us he can fix us to,
he sent his son Jesus to restore us and that's the truth.

Your mess-ups and failures, they have been handled by Jesus,
God sent Jesus to save us is what the bible teaches us.

Jesus showed us the way to become restored,
for whatever the devil has done to us God will undo for sure.

You have a destiny ahead of you and that's no lie,
so rejoice in what God has done in your life,
like opened closed doors that leads to the divine.

It has already been done, your purpose was here before you were
born,
divine destiny has been placed on your life before you were formed.

God places a comma where the devil placed a period,
the devil can't stop anything that God has for you, man that is
serious.

Sometimes when God works in your life you have nothing to say,
just let God fight the battles that comes your way.

Blessed With Poetry

There is a reason for your life, don't fall apart,
say, "I am a real piece of work, I am made from God's own heart."

Job

2: 1-8

This Is Not A Place To Sit

First, know that this scripture is the topic of Job,
but faith is the best topic I suppose.

See, God wants his love in total faith and trust,
not for someone to use when they think common things are enough.

Satan can and will go after his foolish attempt,
to kill, to steal and destroy is what I meant.

So, picture Job sitting on the block of ashes you see,
with sores all over his body from his head to his feet.

This comes after losing his family and all his wealth,
enduring the pain he felt inside, but still knowing God will help.

Job was tested because God allowed Satan to step in,
but God knew his servant Job would have faith until the end.

Is this my dear apart of your faith,
trusting in God and knowing he makes no mistakes?

Now emotions also play a part in this story,
because sometimes emotions take over and kill your faith and glory.

Thinking of Job sitting in this space,
peeling off the sores with scrapes from broken clay.

The pain you feel can't be permanent you see,
you must step out on faith, let life succeed through thee.

Don't let pain sit you down or hold you back,
God said you can't sit here and that's a fact.

Blessed With Poetry

God said I'm with you and I allowed this pain to happen,
to give you strength and lead you like a captain.

This pain that Job felt showed us he still had grace,
so let me ask the question, how strong is your faith?

To rebel against pain and don't let emotions get you down,
move out from that spot and take heed to God's sound.

Did you really think all that Job went through happened in one day,
his family and his wealth was all swept away.

Sometimes it takes us longer to notice what God is doing,
because we think it's all Satan doing the destroying.

But God allows it to move us and show us the way,
the way out of pain that may frustrate us every day.

Why? You may say God allowed this to happen,
to test your faith and see grace present.

So, don't stop where you are don't let that relationship get you
down,
step out on faith because things will come around.

And when it does, start from that point and don't look back,
let God lead you on the right path.

See, God knew the outcome and what Job would do,
God knows our choices and that is true.

God won't let you handle more than you can take,
God knows your strength and how strong you are with faith.

So, get up and don't sit on that hard place full of ashes,
get up out of that pain and look forward to Gods passage.

Blessed With Poetry

Remember, You can't sit here!!!!

Luke

1:39-45

When Believers Come Together

We as Christians are not like everyone else,
the time we spend together should really help.

Help each other through the good and the bad,
feeling God's presence is a joy that we have.

When Christians are together something special should happen,
you should feel God's power, making life feel like heaven.

Jesus healed the sick and gave sight to the blind,
he even calmed the sea with his glory divine.

As Christians you may look like others but inside it can't be true,
for the love you have for God will always come through you.

Through your heart and mind and even on your face,
the pain you feel inside will be replaced.

Replaced with a smile through all your hard times,
my God, no more trouble wondering in your mind.

You see when Elizabeth heard Mary's voice,
the baby inside her jumped and she felt the joy.

That was her confirmation through her pregnancy she knew,
her prayers were answered and she knew this to be true.

So never stop praying because a time will come,
when God will answer your prayers one by one.

When believers get together no matter how many or where,
God will ease your pain and set you up with no despair.

My Wings

Thank You

Thank you for my time here,
thank you Lord for always being near.

This is my time to share my love,
and let my family know that I'm okay up above.

Above the clouds and shining bright,
don't forget my smile for it will give you light.

Yes, I'm here for an eternity, my life hasn't ended,
it's just the beginning.

God just greeted me and told me I'm okay,
I had to summit for his smile showed me the way.

The way out of pain and into the light,
I feel so good family this is out of sight.

I want you to know that being saved will get you here,
accept God and show him your love and he will always be near.

So, thank you God for this time that I've shared,
with my family and friends who showed me they cared.

I know that you all love me, but God loved me best,
and I accept him so clearly above all the rest.

Thank you family and please love one another,
take care and be sweet and always remember others.

Some will watch and some will pray,
others won't understand that this is the way.

The way to heaven and to God's heart,
is to know him and accept him family, give it to God and be smart.

Acts

4:13

Faith That Confirms Your Life

Peter and John had been with Jesus,
for it showed in them with all of their teachings.

Still preaching God's word with no fear but strength,
brought notice to everyone that cared to listen.

Healing of a man, the Jews didn't understand,
healing words so strong from a man.

But the Jews they thought, "What are they speaking?"
Because the Jews knew Peter and John had no teaching.

But yet they spoke with bold, style and grace,
not knowing or caring about their fate.

The Jews wanted to scare them into not speaking God's word,
but little did they know that the word was to be heard.

No matter what the Jews thought or said,
they could not stop these two, so they listened instead.

And when they listened they could not believe,
the bold faith Peter and John had indeed.

Peter announced how the Jews rejected Jesus you see,
with no thought of anything they were bold and believed.

Peter and John believed everything that Jesus said to them,
expressing that they would one day become fishers of men.

For the stone, the Jews thought would hold the two walls so tight,
became the cornerstone of the building in God's sight.

Blessed With Poetry

Without Jesus there would be no church,
without God in our lives everyone would know our hurt.

Jesus and only Jesus can hold us together,
through the pain and hurt he puts it all into perspective.

That is why we can walk with a smile,
just as long as you are with Jesus for just a little while.

Whatever you are hiding God will hold you up,
the time you spend with the word will surely help.

When the Jews saw Peter and John showing boldness and faith,
astonishment fell upon them, they had fearless and elegant ways.

For as ordinary fishermen they spoke like scholars,
Jesus shined through them and when they spoke more followed.

We need to let people know how fearless we can be,
showing our boldness in this world can bring people to their knees.

And don't think that you are an ordinary person for it will show,
the more time spent in the word your strength in God will grow.

Their bold faith in God helped Peter and John take a risk,
to keep speaking Gods word while the Jews wanted them to quit.

The audacity to tell the Jews they were responsible for Jesus death,
"who are these men talking about?" is what their hearts must felt.

Having bold faith comes from the inside out,
for the word inside will shine without a doubt.

But if your faith is only in the world you see,
it will not last long just as all material things.

Blessed With Poetry

Your clothes and cars don't get you bold faith,
but the love of God from inside will show all the way.

Your faith requires an agreement, as you will know,
to serve God which allows your faith to grow.

But, Peter and John stood in court like ambassadors you see,
and did not back down or apologize for saying what they believed.

This was to honor God and what they believed,
so remember only serve the word and not the people you see.

The more knowledge of the word you have the bolder you'll be,
to speak Gods word to others, for you will set them free.

You see, bold faith comes with affirming and association,
God will demonstrate it in your proclamation.

What the Jews saw in the courtyard was a confirmation of the truth,
that Peter and John had been with Jesus and that was true.

The Jews could not doubt what they could truly see,
that Peter and John was Jesus in a different form from thee.

Even though Jesus was not present in his former form,
the word continued to flow forth from those he adorned.

When people want to know how you handle your pain and grief,
tell them it's because of the man who died on Calvary.

But we all know that is not how the story ends,
for he now lives in us when he rose again.

Now, be bold and let your faith confirms,
that the more time you spend in the word the more your boldness
will stand firm.

1 Samuel

2:8

Are you Hannah Or Peninnah?

I ask you ladies who are you,
when your man claims that his love is true.

You see who do you really want to be,
are you the love of his life or the one who fills a need?

When I compare you to this story who might you be,
the one he loves or the one he uses for a deed.

See Hannah was the one Elkanah truly loved,
he knew she couldn't have children, but showed her love.

He treated her well and worried about her a lot,
he didn't want her to be unhappy or even feel left out.

Hannah was taunted by Peninnah you see,
but Peninnah was there to help with his family tree.

He made love to Peninnah with the intent to bare children,
that was her only true job as it is mentioned.

Yet Hannah was different he knew she couldn't bear,
but he loved and cared for her with so much care.

It didn't matter that she didn't bare kids,
he just loved her so much he kept her near.

Now, my question to you is, who are you to thee,
the one that he loves or the one that he uses for a deed?

I would rather be Hannah and be loved unconditionally,
than to be Peninnah and be used only for a need.

Again I say who do you claim to be,
the one he loves or the one he uses indeed?

Genesis

12: 1-3

Being Obedient Brings You Blessings

Abram was told to leave Harran,
to trust in God and take his hand.

So, Abram was obedient and did what was told,
he took his family and lead everyone as a whole.

Being obedient is what will give you blessings,
listening to God and learning a lesson.

As a child you may not understand,
just listen to your parents guiding hand.

As the Nike ad states "Just do it" you see,
when you obey your parents you will never need.

Need anything from an outside source,
for God will lead your parents to hold down the fort.

Obedience is following directions and doing what is told,
it will lead you to righteousness and your blessings will unfold.

But as parents we need to do what is right,
lead by example in our kid's sight.

Train up your child in the way that he should go,
teach your child right and the example will show.

Show other kids the right things to do,
just lead by example and it will become a blessing to you.

Follow what is right, for they will see,
the light that will shine in you will be a blessing indeed.

So parents, watch what you say and watch what you do,
believe me your kids are watching you too.

Sensor the TV and the atmosphere they are in,
for it will help them in the future and lead them out of sin.

Remember, be the parent and not the friend,
for in time that will backfire again and again.

Children are our blessings and we must treat them as so,
listen to God and do what is told.

God blessed Abram for generations you see,
just by being obedient and staying on the path that God leads.

Our kids will be blessed for generations to come,
for as your life is blessed so is everyone's.

Everyone that your child comes in contact with,
will be blessed because you have blessed your kid.

See being obedient will bring blessings to you my friend,
it will bring rewards that you will never be able to hold in.

So remember children you're not a whore or a pimp,
you are Gods children and you are blessed from within.

James

1: 19

Think Before You Speak

God uses trials for everyone to see,
to show us things that will help you and me.

God is a giver of good, perfect and complete,
he will never leave us during our trials for his words are unique.

Unique enough for us to hear,
what he is saying during our time of fear.

So James is telling us to be swift to hear, slow to speak and slow to anger,
because our words may sometimes put us in danger.

We have to know that we can't be solely guided by what we feel,
our response will turn out wrong and that's for real.

There are so many trials that we must adore,
but if we respond positive it will be good for sure.

Talking too much may block what we hear,
listen to what God has for us here.

When we speak in anger, we can't retract,
for those words can hurt someone and that's a fact.

So, let's hear before we speak and have control of what we say,
because words last forever and pain is hard to go away.

The act of obedience and righteousness,
is part of what we are taught from God's holiness.

If any man be in Christ he is a new creature,
because God will restore us and that's what he teaches.

Blessed With Poetry

See Jesus came to us in flesh and dirt,
to show us all out of our own hurt.

God wants us to know it's not over when we crash,
he looks and sees the goodness in us then restores us back on the
right path.

Back to goodness and we will cry no more,
because God will see us through the pain and open closed doors.

So it doesn't matter how many times you crash and burn,
for God will bring us out of our wrong turns.

Talk less and listen more to what God has to say,
and respond to everything in a righteous way.

Whether our wreck be in a relationship, finance or something else,
choose the right way and God will surely help.

This, my dear is not a spiritual gift you see,
it is a choice we make that can last an eternity.

So take the right path, and be quick to hear,
you should listen to everything from far and near.

We should be slow to speak words with our tongue,
because words can hurt everyone.

Be slow to anger for it's a battle you see,
remember, God will fight battles for you and for me.

The Book Of Numbers

You Can Be A Part Of This

God's people should not be in bondage you see,
because God is the one who will set you free.

God makes a way for us to escape,
whatever troubles we can't seem to take.

For if you believe in God he will deliver you,
from pain and strife that may bother you to.

God has a way of making everything better,
the pain you're in and the burdens you carry.

In Numbers, God's plan is exposed in two parts,
directly and indirectly is the way to start.

A plan to make things better in your life and mine,
a plan that has started and will always shine.

Some of us have been a part of the plan and it seems confusing and
hard,
but when you look back and see where you've come from you will
feel like a star.

God used Moses to ease his people out,
out of bondage and pain now that is a reason to shout.

To know that God can bring you through,
whatever life has in store for you.

Some people get their praise on because they know it will happen,
some get their praise on because they have been delivered and are
happy.

Blessed With Poetry

Some get their praise on because they need to shout,
because God has answered them, he brought them out.

But, just because something is over doesn't mean it's done,
this may only be the beginning of that bright sun.

God not only stops some things that are not good,
he brings pain to you so it's understood.

To get ready for the territory he is about to take you to,
it will help you grow in your life and that is true.

We have yet to experience what God has for us here,
a life of perseverance in the future it's clear.

So don't be like the Israelites who always complained,
found fault in everything and sometimes cursed God's name.

Just know that even in all your difficult times,
let grace lead you to the promise land and your life will shine.

2 Kings
4: 1-7

How To Handle Chaos

See chaos can be anything that can shake our lives,
but no one can know the true story of it in our minds.

Chaos can come from nowhere and knock you down,
when your so-called friends are not around.

Not around to lift you or to give you a peace of mind,
your friends will disappear every single time.

You don't have to do anything wrong for chaos to come along,
just know your fight and to whom you belong.

There is a big difference in fighting for you and fighting for The Lord,
for God will show you so much more.

See this woman cried out to Elisha a man of God,
to ask him to help her is what she thought.

You know, it's not that God wasn't there all the time,
in her home was her blessing, she just needed to be led to find.

To find the answers to all her problems that she began to share,
Elisha just made her plainly aware.

Elisha told her to go home and shut the door,
to pour oil in borrowed pots and she poured until there was no more.

Listen, the oil never stopped she just ran out of the borrowed pots,
just a sample for you to remember, that Gods love will never stop.

God will not give you what you want but only what you need,
this is why there were just enough pots for her to fill indeed.

Blessed With Poetry

No more than we can handle, no less than we need to receive,
because more becomes junk and of course wasteful needs.

This is a reason to shout once more,
to know that what God intends to give us is what we can adore.

So the lesson in this text is she was told to shut the door,
and deal with her problems in private once more.

When God tells us something to do, we have to shut the door,
to go to our room and learn what it is for.

Obey what God tells you to do and deal with the fight,
and he will lead you straight into the marvelous light.

So just believe it, even if it seems it's not coming to a light,
it may even seem silly and you may think you can't fight the fight.

But have faith and remember, shut the door and obey,
you will come out on top, just look ahead.

Ahead of your pain and what you thought would eat at you,
just trust in God for he will always see you through.

Go ahead my friend and keep pouring the oil,
for the blessing will come just keep asking for more.

Luke

22:61

If I Knew Then What I Know Now

We all have moments that we regret,
Lord, it's too bad we can't take them all back.

If I knew then what I know now,
some of the friends I have would not be around.

That person I dated, that time that I spent,
would be changed in a moment with no harm intent.

Some family members are crazy and mean us harm,
they'll try to hurt us and bring us down into a storm.

Jesus recognizes that there are some tares in us,
but God still loves us no matter what.

We all have a role in our life and we sometimes give too much,
but there is also a side of selfishness in us.

Satan is always out to mess us up,
turn our lives around and make us do evil stuff.

Stuff that we should not do,
stuff that we'll regret it's true.

So keep a righteous crowd around,
that doesn't cause you stress or make you frown.

We will never reach the right place in life by hanging with the
wrong folks,
but God will be right there to teach us both.

So, don't destroy yourself by the mistakes you have made,
God knows everything under the sun and even in the shade.

Blessed With Poetry

We can't fix it until you face it and that's a fact,
so stay in your lane and face all that crap.

That crap that's from before and that crap that is to come,
for you will end up on top with God being your number one.

Do well, stand strong and have faith,
for God is true and he won't make any mistakes.

When the rooster crows, you know the sun is about to come up,
the start of a brand new day and the start of brand new stuff.

Your problems are about to be over and a new day has come,
if I knew then what I know now, I would have trusted the holy
one.

About The Author

Michelle Smith is an amazing daughter, sister, wife and mother to two beautiful children. She is a native of Baltimore, Md. and was educated in the Baltimore City Public School System. Michelle went on to cosmetology school to pursue her dream and love of styling and art. She has since turned her passion for styling and art into a business in which Classiques Hair Designs was born. Michelle's passion for designing and styling goes far beyond hair. She loves making women feel good about themselves by allowing them to own their own beauty. During her free time, Michelle enjoys riding her motorcycle with childhood friends and family. Over the years, Michelle has embarked upon another one of her passions. She loves writing poetry to inspire others. Her love for spiritual poetry is to tell others about the word of God through her vision. Most of all, Michelle loves spending time with the Lord, family and friends. She always says we need to meet people where they are, in order to bring them up. God doesn't see the physical, mental or material part of you. God sees our hearts and we all should seek God for our purpose.

Made in the USA
Lexington, KY
15 November 2019